A Ti to Sleep

Written by Jo Windsor

Rigby

Some animals sleep
in the day and
wake up at night.
Other animals sleep
at night and wake up
in the day.

Some animals will sleep for a long time every day. But many other animals sleep for a short time.

This manatee is asleep.

Sleeping Times

🐘	3 hours	🐁	12 hours
🦒	2 hours	🐸	14 hours
🐬	7 hours	🐍	16 hours

Some wild animals sleep
for a short time.
Giraffes and elephants
have to eat a lot,
so they can't sleep
for a long time.
They stay awake
to keep safe, too.

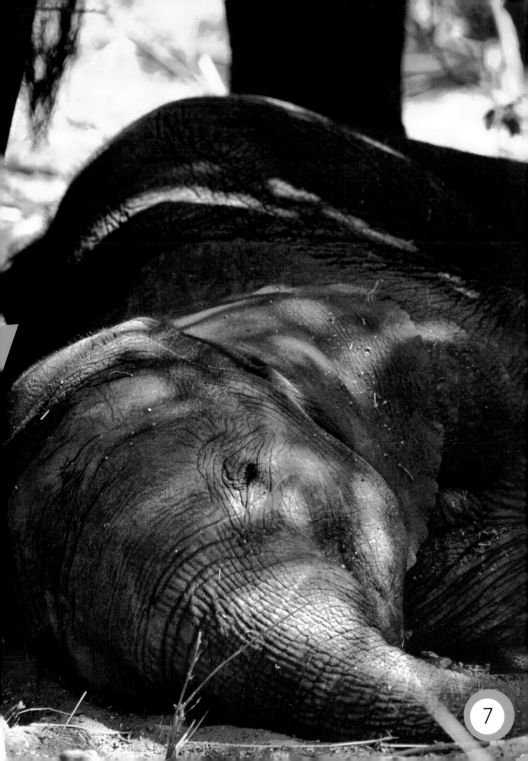

Frogs can sleep
for a long, long time.
They find a hole and sleep
for days and days.

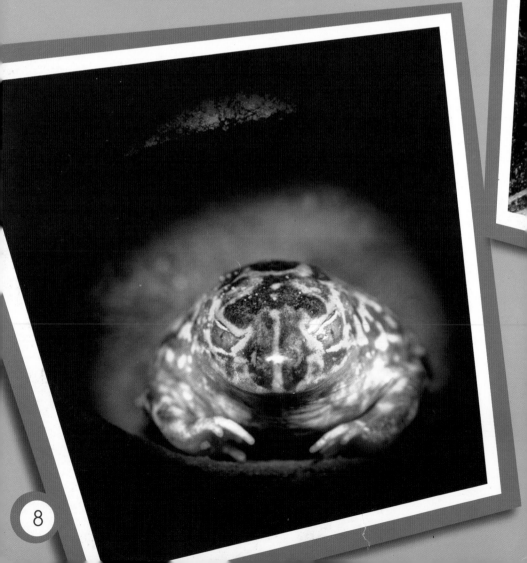

A bear can sleep
for a long time, too.
It will go into a den and
sleep all winter.

Many animals shut their eyes when they go to sleep. Some animals don't shut their eyes at all.

This sea turtle is asleep.

This parrot fish is asleep.

Look at these fish.
They look like they are awake,
but they are asleep.
Their eyes are open.

Look at these snakes.
When they go to sleep,
their eyes stay open, too.

13

Some animals can go to sleep
when they are standing up.
Big elephants
go to sleep standing up,
but little elephants don't!

Index

Guide Notes

Title: A Time to Sleep
Stage: Early (3) – Blue

Genre: Nonfiction
Approach: Guided Reading
Processes: Thinking Critically, Exploring Language, Processing Information
Written and Visual Focus: Photographs (static images), Index, Captions, Comparison Chart
Word Count: 181

THINKING CRITICALLY
(sample questions)

- Look at the front cover and the title. Ask the children what they know about how animals go to sleep and when they go to sleep.
- Focus the children's attention on the index. Ask: "What are you going to find out about in this book?"
- If you want to find out about how long a frog sleeps, what page would you look on?
- If you want to find out about animals that sleep with their eyes open, what pages would you look on?
- Look at pages 2 and 3. Why do you think some animals sleep during the day and some sleep during the night?
- Look at page 9. Why do you think a bear will sleep all winter?

EXPLORING LANGUAGE

Terminology
Title, cover, photographs, author, photographers

Vocabulary
Interest words: wild, awake, sleep, den
High-frequency words: other, many, every, so
Positional words: up, into, in
Compound word: into

Print Conventions
Capital letter for sentence beginnings, periods, commas, exclamation mark